GABBY DAWNAY
ALEX BARROW

If I had a
Sleepy Sloth

I wouldn't want a

I think I'd like a

An  is far too loud

and much too wild, of course!

This sloth belongs to:

· ·

For Bobby – G. D.

For Rachel, Sophie and Emil – A. B.

First published in the United Kingdom in 2020 by
Thames & Hudson Ltd, 181A High Holborn, London WC1V 7QX

First paperback edition 2021

British Library Cataloguing-in-Publication Data
A catalogue record for this book is available from the British Library

ISBN 978-0-500-65262-6

Printed and bound in China by Everbest Printing Co. Ltd

Be the first to know about our new releases,
exclusive content and author events by visiting
thamesandhudson.com
thamesandhudsonusa.com
thamesandhudson.com.au

are bouncy

are very quick.

But I prefer a creature
with a different kind of trick...

People always rush about – I want to stop and stare.

Imagine being so relaxed that moss grew in your hair!

Oh if I had a **sleepy sloth**,
I'd say, 'Hey, what's the rush?

Sit down, relax, my furry friend –
I'll give your hair a brush'.

Sloths are good at gripping.
I think their super-skill
is hanging from the branches
staying seriously still.

If I had a sleepy sloth
we'd watch the world go by
from high up in the jungle
where the treetops meet the sky.

If I had a sleepy sloth we'd walk – but not too fast.

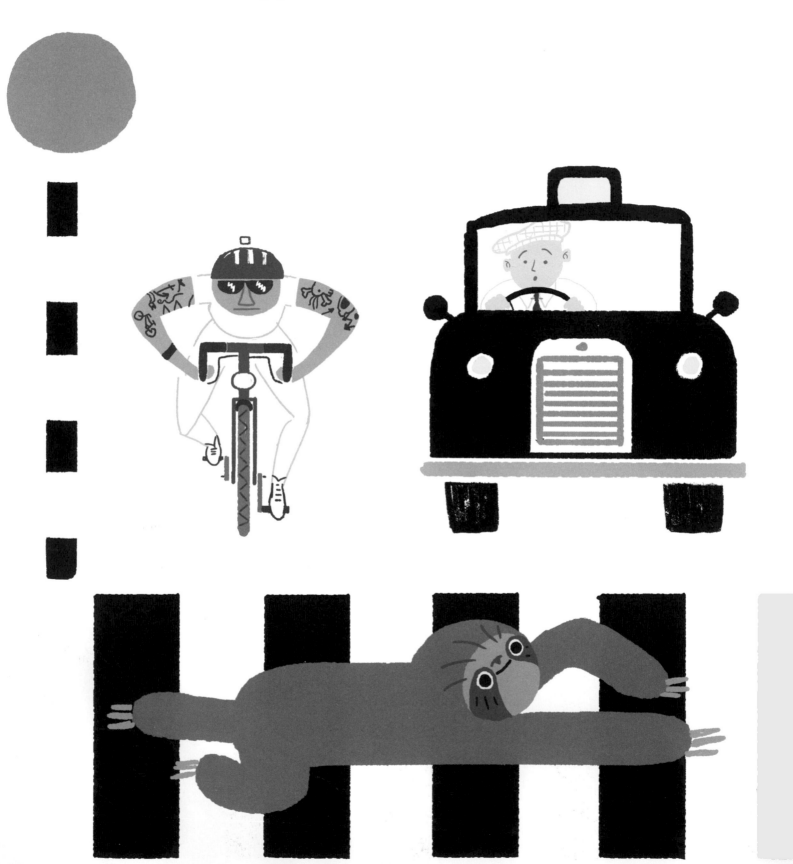

We wouldn't want to race because my sloth would finish last.

Moths are very fond of sloths –
they snuggle in their fur.

If they ever tickled
do you think my sloth would pu-r-rrr?

Sloths are never sweaty, but if it got too hot...

the local pool is very cool – we'd hang out there a lot.

If I had a sleepy sloth
we'd play at hide-and-seek.
(But sloths are so well camouflaged
I'd sometimes have to peek!)

Sloth and I would eat our lunch
while sitting in our tree.

And only once a week my friend
would need to take a...

In our hidden hideaway
we'd never want to leave.

The air would be so fresh up there
we'd close our eyes and b-r-e-a-t-h-e.

Oh if I had a sleepy sloth
I'd have to take things slow.

We'd hang out in a hammock
where we'd watch the flowers grow.

Sloths are very smiley –
they're never, ever down.

(Because they take it easy,
plus, their faces cannot frown.)

I wish I had a sleepy sloth
to cuddle me to sleep.
Then I would count a million sloths
instead of counting sheep!

My sloth would sing a lullaby
and I would close my eyes...
to dream of all the galaxies
way up beyond our skies!

If you'd rather have a giant pet,
you might like to read *If I had a dinosaur*